MY THINK-A-MA-JINK

Written and illustrated by

DAVE WHAMOND

Owl kids

*To my parents, who always inspired me to use my imagination and
to the real life Zac and Maria, who inspire me with their imaginations everyday!*

Owlkids Books Inc.
10 Lower Spadina Avenue, Suite 400, Toronto, Ontario M5V 2Z2
www.owlkids.com

Text and illustrations © 2009 Dave Whamond

Distributed in Canada by Raincoast Books
9050 Shaughnessy Street, Vancouver, British Columbia V6P 6E5

Distributed in the United States by Publishers Group West
1700 Fourth Street, Berkeley, California 94710

Library and Archives Canada Cataloguing in Publication

Whamond, Dave
    My think-a-ma-jink / Dave Whamond.

ISBN 978-1-897349-66-3

    I. Title.

PS8645.H34M9 2009   jC813'.6   C2009-900997-8

Library of Congress Control Number: 2009923336

 Conseil des Arts **Canada Council**
du Canada   for the Arts

 ONTARIO ARTS COUNCIL
CONSEIL DES ARTS DE L'ONTARIO

We acknowledge the financial support of the Canada Council for the Arts, the Ontario Arts Council,
the Government of Canada through the Book Publishing Industry Development Program (BPIDP),
and the Government of Ontario through the Ontario Media Development Corporation's
Book Initiative for our publishing activities.

Printed in China

A   B   C   D   E   F

My name is Jack.
I am bored.

Today was my birthday and I wasn't even that excited. I kept getting toys that did everything for me.

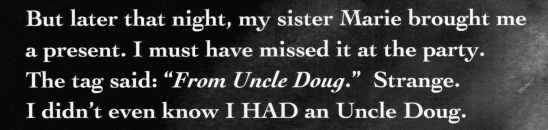

But later that night, my sister Marie brought me
a present. I must have missed it at the party.
The tag said: *"From Uncle Doug."* Strange.
I didn't even know I HAD an Uncle Doug.

We opened the box to find a wonderfully weird
contraption. It looked broken, but shone
like it was brand new.

We found a note, too. It read:

"The Think-a-ma-Jink — an imagination machine. Be anything! Go anywhere! All you have to do is dream."

"I'll believe THAT when I see it,"
I thought as I went to bed.

But I couldn't sleep. That glowing
Think-a-ma-Jink kept me awake.

I needed to try it out.

The instructions said:
"Relax, open your mind,
and repeat the words:

THINK

THINK

THINK-A-MA-JINK

HULLA-BA-LOO

RAZZA-MA-
DOO..."

Boy, did I feel silly. Especially when…
nothing happened!
Just like I thought.

Nope. Nothing. At. All…

Suddenly, I was a freakish mutant monster
attacking an unsuspecting city.
Cool, I've always wanted to do that!

Maybe this thing really worked after all.
All I had to do was think…

And it worked again. The box changed
into a hot air balloon!

This Think-a-ma-Jink could do anything! Like take us to distant corners of the universe to meet far-out crazy aliens.

We could travel to
a time before there
were any humans.

Or I could be a pirate
saving a fair maiden from
a cotton-candy-breathing
dragon. Look out!

I know, I know…it's usually a KNIGHT saving a fair maiden from a FIRE-breathing dragon. But it's MY Think-a-ma-Jink. I can do what I like.

We could even go
to Lollipop-palooza,
where everything was
gooey and delicious!

The only part I didn't like
was getting toffee stuck
between my toes.

We were about to reach the peak of Mount Everfudge when I made the mistake of letting Marie carry the Think-a-ma-Jink.